The
SMUGGLERS of
CRAB COVE

BUNCH OF BADDIES

The SMUGGLERS of CRAB COVE

Andrew Matthews

Illustrated by Guy Parker-Rees

ORCHARD BOOKS

for the staff and pupils of St Margaret
Clitherow School
A.M.
for Sarah and James...Fox!
G.P.R.

ORCHARD BOOKS
96 Leonard Street, London EC2A 4RH
Orchard Books Australia
14 Mars Road, Lane Cove, NSW 2066
1 85213 911 0 (hardback)
1 86039 056 0 (paperback)
First published in Great Britain in 1995
First paperback publication 1997
Text © Andrew Matthews 1995
Illustrations © Guy Parker-Rees 1995
The right of Andrew Matthews to be identified as the Author
and Guy Parker-Rees as the Illustrator of this Work
has been asserted by them in accordance with
the Copyright, Designs and Patents Act, 1988.
A CIP catalogue record for this book is available
from the British Library.
Printed in Great Britain.

CONTENTS

1
THE BUTTON-POLISHING
CHAMPION

Of all the smugglers who ever hoodwinked the Customs men, Blue Fox and his gang were the most irritating. They could land a boatload of French brandy in broad daylight and they could slip through any trap as smoothly as syrup running through a fork. To make matters worse, Blue Fox kept sending short, sarcastic poems to Captain Nazely, the head of the Customs office.

Captain Nazely was bad-tempered at the best of times, but when he arrived at his office one morning and found another poem waiting for him, he went wild. His sidewhiskers bristled and his face turned so red that it filled the air with a rosy glow. He read the poem out loud in a voice choked with fury and thoroughly alarmed Scratter, his private secretary.

"The Customs men search all in vain
Blue Fox, the bold, has struck again"

Captain Nazely ripped up the poem, flung it to the floor and jumped on the pieces, swearing the sort of strong oath that sailors use when they drink cocoa with no sugar in it.

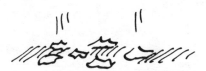

"You seem peeved this morning, sir," Scratter said nervously.

"Peeved?" fumed Captain Nazely. "I'm hopping mad! If Blue Fox isn't caught soon, I may spend the rest of my life bouncing like a kangaroo!"

"Why not give a junior officer a good telling-off, sir?" Scratter suggested tactfully. "You always find it so soothing."

"A capital idea!" agreed Captain Nazely. "Send for Lieutenant Barton!"

Ten minutes later, Brett Barton was standing to attention in front of the captain's desk. He was a fresh-faced young man with curly hair and twinkling blue eyes. He looked so handsome in his uniform that when he walked down the street young ladies swooned, pigeons cooed and cats rolled on the ground, purring loudly.

"You wanted to see me, sir," said Brett, with a smart salute.

"Yes," said Captain Nazely. "I have read your service record, Barton—and it didn't take long. In the three years since you became a Customs officer, you haven't made a single arrest. Why not?"

"Well, er, some of these smuggler types are pretty cunning, sir," Brett explained. "When I try to arrest them, they run away."

Anger made Captain Nazely jiggle about like the lid of a boiling kettle. "Then what have you been doing for the last three years?" he thundered.

"Learning how to polish the brass buttons on my uniform, sir!" Brett replied cheerfully. "In fact, I have won the Customs Officers' Brass-Button-Polishing Championship twice in a row."

Captain Nazely thumped the top of his desk, starting a dusty avalanche of papers.

"Well, you can forget about brass buttons from now on!" he roared. "You're being transferred to our station at Crab Cove. If you haven't caught any smugglers in six weeks' time, I'm going to give you a disgraceful discharge!"

"Don't you mean a dishonourable discharge, sir?" Brett frowned.

Captain Nazely fixed Brett with a look as cold as a penguin on an ice floe. "I mean disgraceful!" he snapped. "Now you'd better go and pack your things. And remember, Barton - six weeks!"

After Brett had left the office, Scratter gazed curiously at Captain Nazely. "Forgive my asking, sir," he said, "but isn't Crab Cove a little on the quiet side?"

"It's quieter than a mousehole with a cat waiting outside it," gloated Captain Nazely. "Lieutenant Barton stands about as much chance of catching a smuggler at Crab Cove as he does of catching a whale with a shrimping net."

"Then...why are you sending him there?" Scratter enquired.

"To make sure he gets discharged!" sniggered Captain Nazely. "Just think, in six weeks, I'll be ripping the precious buttons off his uniform in front of a full parade of Customs officers!" Captain Nazely sighed in a satisfied sort of way. "You know, Scratter," he said, "there are times when I just love this job!"

2

DINNER WITH THE SQUIRE

Crab Cove was a pretty little village, nestling in a sandy bay at the foot of a chalk cliff. Its cottages were neatly whitewashed and so were the church and the inn—*The Queasy Cod*. Several fishing boats bobbed near the shore. It was such an uneventful spot that gulls often fell asleep if they flew overhead, and if a stray dog wandered down the street, people rushed out of doors to gawp at it.

The Customs office was a cottage on the edge of the beach. Brett found himself in command of a leaky rowboat and one other Customs man, Corporal Clem Porlock. Clem was wrinkled and grizzled, and there were so many gaps in his teeth that when he smiled, it looked as though a piano keyboard had been jammed in his mouth.

He gave Brett a tour of the station and proudly showed him the weapons cabinet, which contained a bent cutlass and a rusty musket.

"Is this a busy station?" Brett asked.

"'Tis one mad whirl at times," Clem said. "Why, I got called out only last week! Young Georgie Salmon got 'is fingers stuck in the rowlock of 'is skiff. Tricky job, gettin' 'em out!"

"And, er, what about smugglers?" said Brett.

Clem's laugh sounded like a wet sheet flapping in a gale. "Smugglers?" he chuckled. "Why, I 'as to look the word up in a dictionary to remember what it means!"

"Oh dear!" sighed Brett. "I hope some turn up soon! You see, if I don't catch a smuggler in the next six weeks, I'll be discharged from the Customs service."

"Is that a fact?" said Clem. "Then I reckon as 'ow you're doomed, young sir."

With a heavy heart, Clem glanced out of the window at the sleepy village, and noticed a large house. It was perched on top of the cliff like a condor clinging to a mountain crag. "What's that place?" he said, pointing.

"Wildacres 'All," Clem told him. "It belongs to Squire Twong. There 'ave been

20

Twongs at Wildacres time out of mind."

"It's very impressive," said Brett. "I must take a closer look some time."

"And so you shall!" said Clem, handing Brett a small card. "This came for you earlier."

Always happy to make a new acquaintance. Do come for dinner at Wildacres Hall this evening at seven thirty, cordially yours, Squire Twong

"Seven-thirty!" cried Brett. "I must get ready! Fetch me a clean rag and a bottle of brass-button polish!"

By the time he had finished, Brett's buttons glowed like brass moons. He rode up to Wildacres Hall in the Customs donkey cart, which he parked in the driveway before mounting the front steps and knocking on the door.

The door was opened by a rough-looking fellow with a black patch over one eye and a red handkerchief knotted around his head.

"I'm Lieutenant Barton," Brett explained.

The man's face broke into a sly smile. "Oh, the new Customs man!" he said. "I'm Ripper, the–er–butler. Squire's expectin' you. Just step this way."

Brett followed Ripper into an enormous banqueting hall. There was a long table set for two, and at the far end of the hall a log fire blazed in a white marble fireplace. Standing in front of the fireplace was Squire Twong. He had flowing red hair and a sharp, cunning face.

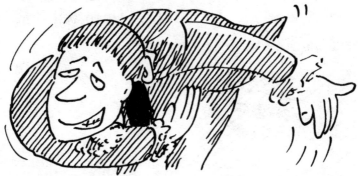

"Welcome to Wildacres Hall, Lieutenant!" said the squire, with an elaborate bow. "I hope you'll protect us from any black-hearted smugglers who might creep into Crab Cove."

"So do I!" said Brett. "You don't know where I can find any, do you? Only I'm anxious to make a quick start in my new post."

Squire Twong threw back his head and laughed until the banqueting hall rang. "Stap me vitals, what a merry wag you are, Lieutenant!" he exclaimed. "I can tell that we're going to get along famously!"

And so they did. Dinner was delicious, as was the wine, and Squire Twong was such a charming host that only when Brett heard the faint chimes of the church clock striking eleven did he realise how late it was.

"I must take my leave," said Brett. "But before I do, there's something I'm rather curious about. I couldn't help noticing the coat of arms embroidered on my napkin."

"My family crest," said Squire Twong. "What of it?"

"Is that a blue dog on the top?" said Brett.

"Some passing whim of one of my ancestors," said Squire Twong with a thin, sharp smile. "Have a safe journey back to the Customs station, dear fellow, and do come again!"

Squire Twong stood at the front door with Ripper beside him and waved to Brett until the donkey cart dipped out of sight along the cliff road.

"Think 'e suspects anythin'?" Ripper muttered.

"Lieutenant Barton is dimmer than a glow-worm in an inkpot!" declared Squire Twong. "So it's business as usual!"

"And what about...Plan X?" whispered Ripper.

"In three days it will be high tide with a full moon," said the squire. "Just right for us to carry out the most daring act of smugglery in the history of crime!"

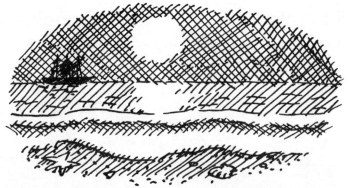

3

LIGHTS ON THE BEACH

Brett couldn't sleep that night. His bedroom was cosy, the bed was comfortable and the sound of the waves breaking on the sand outside was most relaxing—but when he closed his eyes, he saw Captain Nazely's angry face and heard his voice saying, "And remember, Barton—six weeks!"

At last, Brett could stand it no longer. He

got up, slipped into his clothes and went for a walk along the beach to tire himself out. The almost-full moon was high in the sky and it turned the sea to silver. The scene was so calm and beautiful that it made Brett thoroughly miserable.

"How will I ever find any smugglers in a peaceful place like this?" he asked himself glumly. "I may as well give up trying!"

So dismal was Brett's mood, that he walked some distance from the Customs station before he noticed that there were lights moving on the far side of the bay. Several figures holding lanterns were dragging something large across the sand towards the water's edge. The large something was a longboat. The figures pushed it into the sea and climbed aboard. Oars were put out and the longboat began to pull its way across the shining waves.

"Must be the local rowing team!" Brett said softly. "What a dedicated lot, practising at this time of night!"

And then something strange happened. Someone stood up in the front of the boat and waved a lantern from side to side. Far out at sea, another waving light answered it, and Brett made out the shape of a small ship, sailing towards Crab Cove.

"The rowing team must have friends aboard," said Brett. "They're probably going to get together to drink grog and sing rowing songs."

The thought of other people being happy while he was depressed made Brett even more wretched. He walked on, lost in his troubles.

34

He didn't find his way out of them until he reached the place from where the boat had been launched. The footprints in the sand and the long track of the boat's keel led back into the shadows of the cliff.

"Now that's odd!" said Brett. "I can't see a boathouse or cottage anywhere."

He followed the trail up the beach and came to a large cave, lit with flaming torches. Brett entered the cave and found himself in a tunnel that ran deep into the chalk. At the end of the tunnel was a cavern, stacked with barrels and packing cases. There were sacks of spices, crates of vintage wine and bales of rich silks.

"I'd better find out who this belongs to

and have a serious chat with them about home security!" Brett thought.

At the back of the cave was a staircase, carved in the chalk. The steps spiralled up into the darkness.

"I wonder if it goes right to the top of the cliff?" Brett mused. "If it did, it would come out somewhere in the grounds of Wildacres Hall."

He was tempted to climb the stairs and investigate, but he suddenly felt weary. There was a comfortable-looking pile of empty sacks nearby, hidden away behind a small pyramid of brandy casks.

"I think I'll just lie down for a minute." Brett yawned. "I'm sure no one will mind if I have forty winks before I walk back."

But he had more than forty winks. As soon as his head touched the sacks, Brett fell fast asleep.

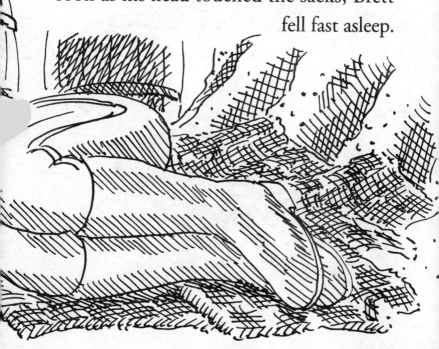

Voices woke him. At first, Brett was too sleepy to understand what the voices were saying, but when he heard the word 'smuggling', it shocked him wide awake. Brett kept as still as a wedge of cheese in a rats' nest.

"So, it's on, then?" said a gravelly, oddly familiar voice.

"Captain Van Tram will make the delivery on Thursday at midnight," said a second voice—and Brett seemed to know this voice too, though he couldn't place it.

"I don't trust that Captain Van Tram!" said a third voice, the most maddeningly familiar of all. " 'E's too Dutch for my likin'!"

"We're in too deep to back out now!" the second voice replied sharply. "This isn't just another boatload of contraband hooch—this is Plan X! We're talking pride of place in the Smuggling Hall of Fame! Now, let's get back to the house for some rest. We've got an early start tomorrow, and I haven't felt so tired since the last time I was this tired!"

Darkness fell as the torches were snuffed out, and then Brett heard footsteps climbing the spiral staircase into silence.

When he was sure he was safe, Brett crept out of the cave and sprinted back across the beach towards the Customs station. His mind was racing faster than his feet.

"So," he thought, "there *are* smugglers at Crab Cove! Well, I mean to nab them red-handed! With a bit of luck, Captain Nazely won't be giving me a disgraceful discharge– he'll be presenting me with a medal!"

4

SWORDS ON THE SAND

Next morning, when Brett told Clem what had happened the night before, he was dismayed to find that the old corporal didn't believe him. "Smugglers–at Crab Cove?" Clem scoffed. "You must 'ave 'ad a few too many up at Wildacres 'All, young sir."

"But it's true!" Brett insisted. "I fell asleep in that big cave under the cliffs, and then–"

"What, Mermaid's Grotto?" Clem interrupted. "You don't want to go near that place. They say 'tis 'aunted!"

"It's not haunted, it's a treasure chamber of smugglers' loot!" exclaimed Brett. "If you come with me, I'll show you!"

But when they got to the cave, there was nothing—no tracks in the sand, no boat, no crates, just mocking shadows and the dripping of water from the clammy walls.

"They must have come back and moved it," said Brett. "That's it...at first light they must have sneaked back here, and—"

"If you take my advice, you'll lie down and take things easy, young sir," Clem said gravely. "I reckon as 'ow you've got a touch of management stress, brought on by too much responsibility."

"D'you think it might all have been a dream, then?" Brett mumbled in confusion.

"Ah, that's right—'twas just a dream!" said Clem. "Now you go back to the station for a nice, long rest, and forget all about smugglers!"

Brett stayed in his bedroom all day, thinking long and hard. Despite what Clem had said, he was sure that the smugglers had been real. He made up his mind to go back to Mermaid's Grotto on Thursday night–and since Clem obviously wouldn't come with him, he would have to go alone.

The next few days passed quietly. Brett unlocked the arms cabinet and more or less straightened the cutlass, but the musket was beyond repair. The butt was so riddled with woodworm that it fell to dust as soon as he picked it up.

"I'll have to depend on surprise," Brett told himself, "and hope that the smugglers can't run faster than I can."

On Thursday night, while the villagers of Crab Cove were tucked up in their beds, snugger than fleas in a fleece, Brett hid behind a chalk boulder near the mouth of Mermaid's Grotto. He waited until his limbs ached. He began to wonder if it really had been a dream after all. "I'm glad I didn't tell anyone else about this," he thought. "I must look a real fool crouching behind this boulder in the middle of the night!"

The minutes crawled by like walruses on land. The church clock struck eleven, then quarter past—but when it chimed the half-hour, things started to happen.

Three men with lanterns came out of the cave, hauling a longboat behind them.

They were wearing hooded cloaks, with
the hoods pulled well down to conceal
their faces. They launched the boat and
rowed out to sea. At first, Brett couldn't
tell where they were headed, but then the
full moon came out from behind a cloud
and it was almost as bright as day. There
was the ship Brett had spied before. A
light signalled to the longboat, and in a
few minutes the two vessels were
alongside.

It was too far for Brett to see, but whatever the smugglers were up to took a long time. Not until it was almost one o'clock did the longboat head for shore, and its crew seemed to be having some difficulty rowing. Whatever they had on board was large, thin and tall.

Brett had to wait until the longboat beached in the surf before he could recognise the cargo, and when he did he was completely astonished. Standing in the centre of the boat, clearly lit by the moon, was...

At first, Brett could only open his mouth wider and wider as the smuggler gang struggled to get the animal ashore. Then he remembered his duty. He took a firm grip on his cutlass, stood upright and strode down the beach.

The smugglers wheeled around. The hood of the tallest man fell back, and Brett saw his face.

"All right, Blue Fox, what are you doing with that ostrich?" Brett asked sternly.

"Smuggling it into the country to sell to the highest bidder," said Squire Twong. "There's many a rich man with a private zoo who would pay a pretty penny for a fine bird like this! Any fool can smuggle wine or silk, but smuggling an ostrich takes genius!"

"Your life of crime is at an end!" Brett declared. "You and your gang are under arrest for smuggling an endangered species!"

"I don't think so!" hissed Squire Twong, drawing his rapier and swishing it through the air. "I thought we'd managed to put you off the scent, Lieutenant, but you're more stubborn than I thought! I see you're holding a cutlass. Can you use it?"

"Not a lot," Brett admitted.

"A pity!" sneered Squire Twong. " I am one of the finest swordsmen in the land.

For example, how about this?"

Squire Twong lunged, his sword f l a s h e d , a n d something fell to the sand at Brett's feet.

Brett looked down and saw that a brass button was missing from his jacket. "You fiend!" he cried. "I hate it when anyone spoils my uniform—especially the buttons!" He was so angry that he forgot to feel afraid. He raised his cutlass and before long he was in the middle of a wing-ding swordfight.

There was a lot of ringing steel and grunting. Brett and Squire Twong came face to face over their locked blades and traded frightful insults—but for all his courage, Brett was completely outclassed.

In fact, things might have gone badly if the ostrich hadn't lent a hand—or at least a claw. The poor beast was so fed up with being pushed and pulled that it lost its temper and lashed out with its left leg.

The kick landed squarely in the seat of Squire Twong's britches. The squire rose a metre or so in the air, and then came down with a thud that made the ground shake and knocked him senseless.

The other smugglers gave up without a fight. One of them was Ripper and the other turned out to be Clem Porlock.

"Clem!" said Brett, deeply shocked. "How could you?"

"'Tis the old, old story!" Clem sighed sorrowfully. "A poor 'ome background drove me to want revenge on society—and of course, the money came in 'andy!"

Under Brett's watchful eye, Ripper and Clem carried Squire Twong to the local constable's office, where they were held under guard until a carriage arrived to take them to the nearest gaol.

There was a sensational trial, and the gang were sentenced to years and years of community service at the municipal rubbish tip.

The ostrich was confiscated by the Crown, and returned to its rightful home on the plains of Africa by a team from the Royal Zoological Society.

As for Brett, he received such a handsome reward for capturing Blue Fox that he left the Customs service and went to live at Crab Cove. There his eye was caught by the innkeeper's daughter, Sophie. Before too long, they married—and if they didn't exactly live happily ever after, they came as close as you can get.

Here are another *Bunch of Baddies* for you to read…

CAPTAIN MIDNIGHT AND
THE GRANNY BAG
Stand and deliver! On Hangman's Heath the dastardly
highwayman Captain Midnight lies in wait to rob the
Royal Mail coach …but tonight he's in for a shock.

THE CACTUS BOYS
The toughest, meanest and fastest-shooting outlaws in
the Old Wild West are the Cactus Boys …until they
meet the sheriff of Lavender Gulch…

GALACTACUS THE AWESOME
Sam Brassworthy wasn't really expecting to be whisked
on board an alien spaceship. But now it's up to him to
save the Earth from the most terrifying monster from
outer space.

THE VOYAGE OF THE PURPLE PRAWN
Hoist the sails and set course for Parrot Isle and buried
treasure with blackhearted Abel Thinscratch and his
pirate crew.